Miniphant & Me

The Magnificent Raspberry Mountain

Cally Gee

CWR

PRINTED MAY 2018

Editing, design and production by CWR.
Cover image: Cally Gee and CWR.
Printed in the UK by Linney.
ISBN: 978-1-78259-839-8

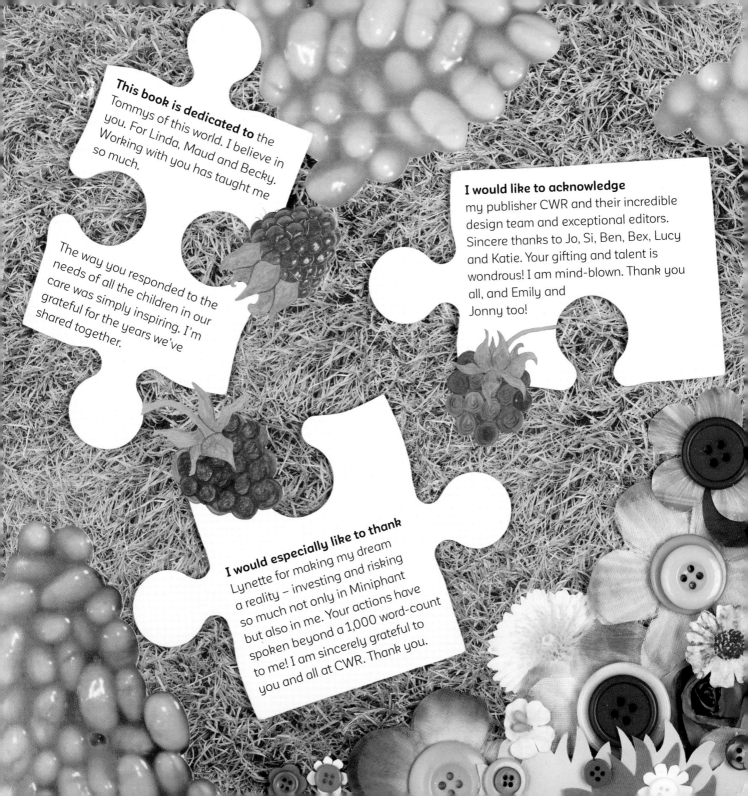

This book is dedicated to the Tommys of this world. I believe in you. For Linda, Maud and Becky. Working with you has taught me so much.

The way you responded to the needs of all the children in our care was simply inspiring. I'm grateful for the years we've shared together.

I would like to acknowledge my publisher CWR and their incredible design team and exceptional editors. Sincere thanks to Jo, Si, Ben, Bex, Lucy and Katie. Your gifting and talent is wondrous! I am mind-blown. Thank you all, and Emily and Jonny too!

I would especially like to thank Lynette for making my dream a reality – investing and risking so much not only in Miniphant but also in me. Your actions have spoken beyond a 1,000 word-count to me! I am sincerely grateful to you and all at CWR. Thank you.

Dear Mini Friend,

Hello! Welcome to another **Miniphant & Me** book.

My friends and I are so excited to share our adventures with you!

Our stories talk about:

thoughts in our head...

feelings in our heart...

and actions with our body...

because the way we think changes the way we feel and what we choose to do.

See if you can spot these in the story!

As you might have guessed by now, I love food, but in today's story I get myself into quite a mess over it! You will soon see how my feelings shaped my thoughts, which then affected my actions – sometimes in a bad way.

We all get grumpy, frustrated and angry at times, but it's what we do with those feelings that makes all the difference. If we can spot how they show up in our bodies, we can learn to control our feelings (with our thoughts and actions) instead of letting our feelings control us! This helps us to stay calm and put things right, instead of landing in a mushy mess like I did!

There's also some more Bedtime Thoughts and Daytime Fun at the back of the book – I'll come and find you at the end of the story to tell you more about them. Have fun!

Love, **Miniphant** x

One last thing... raspberries end up everywhere in this story! Can you find them all?

Miniphant began his day doing 'trumpercise'.

After five whole minutes of trumping (out of both ends), exercise soon turned to thoughts of food.
'I'm hungry!' he said, squeezing through the crack in the shed door.

'Good morning, Miniphant,' Robin sang.

'Can't stop, Robin!' replied Miniphant, jogging straight past Robin's tree in search of food.

'I have a hungry tummy and have run out of my favourite food!'

he panted.

'There are lots of juicy raspberries at the bottom of the garden. I could fly over to get you some?'

Robin called.

'Mmmm, raspberries!' thought Miniphant as he trotted on, too busy dreaming of food to listen to Robin's kind offer.

(Choosing to stop and listen would have been a very helpful thing to do at this moment.)

Cat came purring along, making Miniphant sneeze.

Feeling annoyed, Miniphant flapped his ears and powerwalked on as fast as his little legs could go.

'Sorry, Miniphant!' Cat meowed after him. (She was trying very hard to practise saying 'sorry' when she should.)

'I was going to offer to help you...'

But Miniphant could think of nothing but the juicy raspberries ahead.

Suddenly, Mole dug a big hill right in front of him. Miniphant trumped loudly out of both ends, without even saying, 'Oopsie-poopsie-pardon'!

'MOLLLLLLLLLE!' Miniphant spluttered, as dirt flew up his trunk.

'Whoops! I'm sorry, Miniphant. I didn't mean to cover you with dirt.' Mole felt terrible when she realised that she had upset her friend, even though it was an accident. She wanted to find a way to make it up to him.

'Why the hurry?' she asked.

'I'm REALLY hungry!' he stomped, clambering over the molehill.

Mole tried to help, but Miniphant didn't want help. He wanted <u>food</u>!

By the time Miniphant arrived at the raspberry bushes, his tummy was rumbling like a giant oopsie-poopsie-pardon about to explode, as well as feeling rather tired from running the length of the garden. He looked up in amazement at all the fat, mouth-wateringly juicy raspberries above him. They looked BEAUTIFUL! But he couldn't reach them!

Growing hotter and crosser, Miniphant wasn't just *hungry* anymore. He was also becoming VERY angry...

Miniphant was **H A N G R Y !**

Mole appeared next to him, and seeing Miniphant's gritted teeth and snorting breaths, she desperately wanted to help. She had a wonderful helping idea, but didn't think to tell Miniphant about it – she just started digging again without any warning!

Covered by another shower of dirt, Miniphant – eyes wide and fists clenched – shouted,

'WHAT ARE YOU DOING???'

The dirt pile rose higher and higher until it seemed as tall as a mountain. Mole popped her head out the top.

'Climb up, Miniphant, and see if you can reach the berries now!'

Miniphant had no words.

He didn't know what was happening.

Huffing and puffing, he scrambled upwards,

his thoughts all muddled

and out of control.

Arriving at the top, Miniphant could see he was getting closer to reaching the raspberries, but he still wasn't close enough.

'Perhaps try standing on your suitcase too?' Mole suggested.

Cat jumped up to join them.

'What are you doing nooow?' she meowed.

'We're trying to reach the raspberries — to stop Miniphant's tummy from being hungry!' sighed Mole.

'He makes enough "raspberries" of his own,' Cat replied. 'He doesn't need any more!'

Miniphant's hangry feelings took over, and he started trumping like a herd of elephants, shouting out orders:

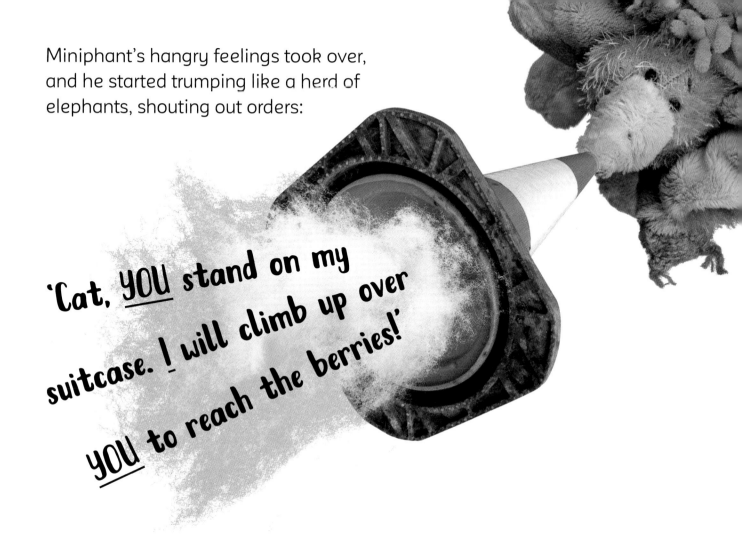

'Cat, <u>YOU</u> stand on my suitcase. <u>I</u> will climb up over <u>YOU</u> to reach the berries!'

His 'hanger' was making him forget how to treat others.

Cat decided to ignore his rude and bossy tone and remain calm, knowing that food would help Miniphant to feel better and think more clearly about his actions. It was very brave of Cat to allow anything to touch her fur, but she knew this was a good chance to practise being kind and selfless.

Just as Cat, Mole and Miniphant got into position, down flew Robin, landing among the very raspberries they were trying to reach!

Miniphant went **RAGE RED**, remembering that not only could Robin **fly**, but he had offered to help him in the first place! If only he had listened to Robin! He trumped angrily at himself, out of both ends (much to Cat's complete disgust below).

'Miniphant!' said Robin firmly, 'I know you are hungry, and I have an idea of how we can help you. But the way you are feeling, thinking and acting is not kind or helpful to anyone. We are all here to help, but you need to stop and do some good listening so that you can play your part in us all working together. And speaking of working together, perhaps you could remember <u>not</u> to do oopsie-poopsie-pardons in your friends' faces!'

Miniphant found it hard, hearing the truth about his behaviour. He went quiet, thinking about what he had done. Grumpily sniffing back tears, he told his hangry feelings to wait, and made the very good choice to listen to Robin and his idea.

The raspberry wobbled.

Miniphant wobbled.

Robin's plan worked. Before long, there was a **Magnificent Raspberry Mountain** below. Miniphant could hardly wait to EAT!

But just as Robin passed him the final and biggest berry, his tummy gave another GIANT **rumble**, and he couldn't hold the berry still to roll it down Cat's back to Mole.

Cat wobbled.

The suitcase wobbled.

Squelch!

Raspberries flew everywhere – along with Miniphant!

Mole, Cat and Robin looked at each other, then looked down.

Below them, a shocked, BRIGHT PINK Miniphant lay in a mushy mess of squashed raspberries, making sounds of his own.

He. Felt. Dreadful.

He knew he had let his hanger reach boiling point.

'What a mess I've made! Oopsie-poopsie-pardon-me, I'm so sorry! You have all been very kind and patient, while I let myself become angry, rude and selfish. Please forgive me!'

Relieved that Miniphant could finally see the mess his hanger had created, the three friends lovingly smiled back in forgiveness.

'Berry smoothie, anyone?'

Miniphant slurped, trying to make something good out of the chaos he'd caused.

Stop and think.
Switch on listening ears.
Take big slow breaths.

When everyone was full, Miniphant wrote all he had learnt inside his suitcase. He was feeling very thankful for friends who showed care and kindness towards him – even when he had forgotten to be kind and caring himself. They also encouraged him to keep 'trumpercising' – as long as he had a baked bean sandwich ready for afterwards.

Say sorry and make things right.

The sun was going down, and it felt good to have done some hard pond for a swim, the friends helped Miniphant to wash the good lessons he had learned and packed in his

thinking about all that had happened. Wandering down to the away the raspberry stains, until all that remained were suitcase, ready for him to carry into a new day.

Bedtime Thoughts and Daytime Fun

Hello again, Mini Friend!

I hope you enjoyed the story. What a lot of raspberries!

What changes did you notice in my body, voice, words and actions, showing that I was becoming angry? What things happened to make me act this way?

What were all my friends trying to do for me? That's right! They were trying to help me! I learnt that I need to practise listening and accepting help from others. Here are some more really helpful things we can learn together.

Bedtime Thoughts

Grown-ups: you can use these thinking, whispering and listening activities as part of the bedtime routine, enhancing your child's emotional literacy, mental health and spiritual wellbeing. They are designed to be calming and settling, thought provoking and comforting at the end of the day.

Emotional Literacy

To talk about

Anger is a feeling that comes to visit sometimes, just like other feelings do. Feelings try to tell you how things are or how they seem, but do you want to know a secret? Well, here it is: *feeling* something doesn't always mean it's true. So we need to *think* through our feelings and decide how we will act. Anger is a feeling that needs to be taken care of, because it can make all sorts of trouble if we let it.

Figuring out why you are angry is a good place to start. Angry feelings can be like a mask – they hide other feelings that are going on inside us. We need to be brave and find those hidden feelings and share them with someone we trust (like the grown-up reading this book), so that we can understand what is making us feel this way, and what we can do to make things better.

To do

Think about something that happened that made you feel angry. Bravely whisper together what that was and why you felt that way. Were any other feelings hiding behind your angry ones?

Go ahead and whisper them into each other's ear. Then think up some happy and helpful thoughts to say into your pillow as you fall asleep.

Mental Health

To talk about

The more you think thoughts that are good, true and helpful, the less angry you'll feel and the more settled you'll remain. It's *how* you think about something that makes your anger grow. If you keep thinking angry thoughts, you'll become more and more angry.

Try thinking differently about what is making you feel angry. Your thoughts belong to you. Did you know that YOU are the BOSS of how you think and feel about things? You are! So you get to tell your mind what you want it to think about. And then you can tell your body and words what you want them to do and say. In the Animal Friend Fact Files on the website, the animals share about what anger looks like in their bodies, and how they make it go away. You could have a look at these, then make your own fact file!

To do

What do you do when your anger wants to visit? What does your body or voice do? Talk about these things together. What could you do differently that would help you look after your angry feelings better? Try to come up with some ideas that will help. Tomorrow, you could try doing some of the things the animals do on the website.

Spiritual Wellbeing

To talk about

Miniphant's friend Jesus tells us in His book, the Bible, that He knows what it's like to feel angry because there were times when He was angry Himself. His stories teach us how we can learn to live happily together, alongside all our coming and going feelings, because His never-ending love for us is always there, always the same and does not change. All the feelings in the whole world can't make Jesus love you any more or any less than He already does. His love is not based on how **you** feel but on what **He** says about you. And He says you are lovable **ALL** the time.

It's because of Jesus' love for you that He encourages you to sort out anything that has made you angry before you go to bed – otherwise you won't sleep very well and all those unhappy feelings will still be there when you wake up, making you sad the next day too. No one wants to wake up sad!

To do

Before going to sleep now, is there anything from today that you need to talk about? Do you need to say sorry for something? Or perhaps you need to forgive someone else? Sort out and put right. Do it and you'll feel much better – ready to start a brand-new day tomorrow.

Daytime Fun

Grown-ups: these activities are designed to be interactive, fun and creative and can be integrated into your child's day to enhance their physical awareness, social understanding and creative thinking.

Physical Activity: 'When anger visits, the Boss says...' (along the lines of 'Simon says')

Because our angry feelings often show themselves through our bodies, we can teach our bodies how to help us by learning lots of ways to look after ourselves, each other and our belongings. Remember, anger comes to *visit* but it doesn't have to stay. Miniphant packs his suitcase with thoughts he wants to remember. We can do this too, by imagining that our heads are suitcases where we can keep helpful thoughts with helpful actions. Remember, *you are the boss of your feelings!*

Player 1 ('The Boss') says 'I'm the Boss! And when anger visits, the Boss says...' (calls out different anger-releasing actions, which the other players carry out).

eg 'I'm the Boss! And when anger visits, the Boss says to find a safe space / take time out!'

Other players act this out, eg curling up on the floor / sitting in a corner with a book etc

Call: move! / Action: dance on the spot / do star jumps / shake like a jelly

Call: walk away! / Action: walk in another direction

Call: sleep! / Action: lie down on the floor

Call: eat! / Action: pretend to eat a piece of fruit

Call: talk about it! / Action: pretend to talk to someone

Call: ask for a hug / Action: pretend to give someone a hug

Call: breathe! / Action: take deep breaths in and out

Call: count! / Action: count on fingers

(Grown-ups: you can repeat the same instructions multiple times. The more these behaviours are practised, the more likely the children will remember them the next time they feel angry. Making it a fun, interactive activity shows that anger is just a part of life but that there are helpful ways to look after anger when it comes to visit.)

Social Activity: What Happens Next?

After anger has gone away and you are able to think and talk calmly about what happened, putting things right again is an important part of ending anger's visit.

If your words or actions have hurt someone else, it's important to say sorry for hurting them and think if there's anything else you can do to make things better.

If someone else has hurt you, it's important to forgive them so that you can let go of those hurt feelings and move on to happier things.

Do you need to forgive someone? Write their name on a piece of paper and say out loud, 'I forgive you (their name) for (the hurtful thing they did or said).' Screw the paper up and throw it in the bin as a way of letting your hurt go, and carry forgiveness in your thoughts instead. Then go and do something fun!

Do you need to say sorry to someone? If they are nearby, go and tell them that you are sorry and why you are sorry. If they have gone away, draw them a picture of something you know they like and send it to them, asking an adult to help you write why you are sorry. Then go and do something fun!

(Grown-ups: praise the child every time they take care of their anger feelings, or do something to restore relationship, especially when done without prompting. Model how you constructively manage your own anger feelings – tell them what you are doing to stay calm and how you also put things right. Modelling humility to them will build their confidence to try it too.)

Creative Activity: Make your own Magnificent Raspberry Mountain!

Make some raspberries using modelling clay. Find a small, clear container and draw a triangle on the front to make it look like a mountain. (Grown-ups: every time your child shows that they are looking after their anger feelings, they can put a raspberry in the mountain pot and watch it grow into their own Magnificent Raspberry Mountain! As soon as a raspberry reaches the top, reward their progress by making a smoothie with real raspberries. They will literally be enjoying the 'fruit' of their helpful thinking!)

Other anger management tools:

- Sensory play, such as using your hands with modelling clay, baking, sand or water can be very helpful ways of calming down and relaxing. It can also provide an opportunity for conversation and further learning to be had while playing.
- Create a safe space or a time-out corner with cushions, blanket, books.
- Make a Raspberry Rewards Chart that reinforces positive behaviour and good choices made throughout the day.

More tips and resources for helping children manage their feelings can be found at **www.cwr.org.uk/miniphant**

It's time to say goodbye now! It has been great fun being with you again! Come and join me and my friends for more adventures in our other books.

See you **oopsie-poopsie** soon!
Love,

Miniphant x

Join Miniphant and friends for more adventures in

Miniphant Moves In
and
One Big Adventure

For more information about the **Miniphant & Me** series,
including additional Bedtime Thoughts, Daytime Fun and lots more, visit

www.cwr.org.uk/miniphant